To Nikki

Never stop believing in yourself!

♡ Tracey Gene

RUBY CHRISTMAS | RUBY'S FIRST CHRISTMAS

ISBN 978-0-578-42802-4

PUBLISHED BY TRACEY GENE
AUTHOR AND ILLUSTRATOR: TRACEY GENE

WWW.RUBYCHRISTMAS.COM

FOR JAKE.
WHO BELIEVED IN ME AND FOR LISTENING TO ALL OF MY CHRISTMAS STORIES.
THANK YOU FOR MAKING THIS BOOK POSSIBLE.

ONCE UPON A TIME, ON A SNOWY CHRISTMAS DAY...

...THE LIFE OF SANTA'S TOP REINDEER WAS ABOUT TO CHANGE...

...AND IT STARTED WITH THE MERRIEST OF NEWS.

HE WAS BLESSED WITH A BABY GIRL...

WHO HAD SNOW-FRECKLES THAT TWINKLED SLIGHTLY...

...AND A HEART-SHAPED NOSE THAT GLOWED SO BRIGHTLY.

SHE WAS A BEAUTY...

...AND SO, HE DECIDED TO CALL HER HIS LITTLE RUBY.

AS LITTLE RUBY GREW UP, SHE WOULD VISIT HER DAD AT PRACTICE...

...HER LITTLE HEART-SHAPED NOSE WOULD GLOW EVEN BRIGHTER WHEN SHE SAW HIM FLYING...

...AND THAT'S WHEN SHE KNEW, SHE WANTED TO GROW UP TO BE JUST LIKE HER DAD!

LITTLE RUBY COULD NOT WAIT FOR SCHOOL TO START...

...TO MEET ALL OF THE OTHER REINDEER AND TO LEARN HOW TO FLY!

WHEN LITTLE RUBY FINALLY STARTED SCHOOL...

...ALL OF THE OTHER REINDEER WANTED TO BE HER FRIEND BECAUSE OF HER BRIGHT HEART-SHAPED NOSE!

LITTLE RUBY LEARNED ABOUT CHRISTMAS AND ALL OF THE OTHER DUTIES REINDEER HAD TO PLAY...

...RUBY COULD NOT WAIT FOR HER FIRST FLYING CLASS THAT WAS SCHEDULED MIDDAY.

THE TEACHER TOLD THE LITTLE REINDEER THAT THE MOST IMPORTANT PART IS BELIEVING...

...AND TO START RUNNING...

...AS LITTLE RUBY AND THE OTHER REINDEER STARTED TO RUN, THEY SHOUTED AS LOUD AS THEY COULD, SAYING

" I BELIEVE."

ALL THE OTHER REINDEER STARTED TO FLY AND SHOUTED WITH GLEE!

EXCEPT FOR LITTLE RUBY...

...AS RUBY TRIED AND TRIED, SHE STARTED TO CRY...

...AND THEN, ALL OF A SUDDEN, HER BRIGHT HEART-SHAPED NOSE WENT OUT...

...BUT SHE DIDN'T POUT.

AS LITTLE RUBY GOT HOME, SHE TOLD HER DAD THAT SHE TRIED AND TRIED, BUT COULDN'T FLY AND ALL OF THE OTHER REINDEER STARTED TO TEASE HER.

HE TOLD HIS RUBY NOT TO LISTEN TO THE OTHER REINDEER...,
...AND THAT PRACTICE MAKES PERFECT...

... PLUS, YOU HAVE TO BELIEVE IN YOURSELF...

... AND TO NEVER GIVE UP ON YOUR DREAMS TO FLY.

SO, THAT'S WHAT LITTLE RUBY DID...

SHE PRACTICED EVERY SINGLE DAY.

ON THE DAY OF CHRISTMAS EVE...

...SANTA WAS TOLD THAT HIS TOP REINDEER BROKE HIS LEG AND THAT HE COULDN'T HELP GUIDE HIS SLEIGH THAT NIGHT!

AS SANTA STARTED TO WONDER WHO COULD GUIDE HIS SLEIGH...

...HE SPOTTED LITTLE RUBY IN THE CANDY CANE FOREST
THAT WAS FAR AWAY...

...CURIOUS, SANTA WAS...

...SO, HE HEADED
HER WAY.

WHEN SANTA ASKED LITTLE RUBY WHAT SHE BEEN UP TO...

...SHE TOLD HIM SHE WAS PRACTICING TO FLY, BECAUSE SHE WANTS TO BE LIKE HER DAD AND BE PART OF HIS TOP REINDEER.

SANTA TOLD LITTLE RUBY SHE NEEDS TO BELIEVE IN HEART THAT SHE CAN DO ANYTHING SHE WANTS...

...AND OF COURSE, CLOSE HER EYES AND CLICK HER FRONT TWO HOOVES TOGETHER, TWICE!

...SO SHE DID...

WHEN LITTLE RUBY OPENDED HER EYES...

...SHE SHOUTED WITH GLEE!

LITTLE RUBY WAS FLYING...

...AND SHE WAS HAPPY AS SHE COULD BE!

WHEN LITTLE RUBY LANDED ON THE GROUND...

...SANTA ASKED HER IF SHE WOULD SAVE CHRISTMAS BY GUIDING HIS SLEIGH TONIGHT.

MOMENTS BEFORE SANTA WAS TO LEAVE...

...SANTA'S TOP HELPERS NOTICED HE WAS MISSING, ALONG WITH HIS TOP REINDEER!

WHEN SANTA MAGICALLY APPEARED...

...EVERYONE STARTED TO CHEER!

...UNTIL, SANTA TOLD EVERYONE THAT LITTLE RUBY IS GOING TO SAVE CHRISTMAS BY GUIDING HIS SLEIGH TONIGHT!

EVERYONE STARTED WHISPERING...

"HOW CAN THAT BE?"

"DOES SANTA NOT KNOW THAT RUBY CANNOT FLY!?"

SHE THOUGHT...RUBY'S NOSE IS BRIGHT RED AGAIN!!

SANTA GOT IN HIS SLEIGH AND SAID "HO HO HO. RUBY LET'S MAKE THIS A GREAT CHRISTMAS!"

LITTLE RUBY SAID "YOU GOT IT. SANTA!"

AS RUBY BEGAN TO RUN. SHE TOOK OFF FROM THE GROUND. AS DID THE OTHER REINDEER. AND SANTA AND HIS SLEIGH!

EVERYONE STARTED TO SHOUT WITH GLEE...

...AND KNEW LITTLE RUBY WOULD FOREVER CHANGE HISTORY!!

CPSIA information can be obtained
at www.ICGtesting.com
Printed in the USA
BVHW022128240619
551884BV00006B/15/P

9780578428024